HOUSTON ROCKETS

ALL-TIME GREATS

BY BRENDAN FLYNN

Book design by Jake Slavik
Cover design by Jake Slavik

Photographs ©: Michael Wyke/AP Images, cover (top), 1 (top); Rick Bowmer/AP Images, cover (bottom), 1 (bottom); George Long/Sports Illustrated/Set Number: X15345 F7/Getty Images, 4; Focus on Sport/Getty Images Sport/Getty Images, 7; Focus on Sport/Getty Images, 9; Allsport/Getty Images Sport/Getty Images, 10; James Nielsen/AFP/Getty Images, 13; Andy Hayt/Sports Illustrated/Set Number: X25465/Getty Images, 14; Sporting News/Getty Images, 16; John W. McDonough/Sports Illustrated/Set Number: X44076/Getty Images, 17; Greg Nelson/Sports Illustrated/Set Number: X162642 TK1/Getty Images, 18; David J. Phillip/AP Images, 20; Adam Glanzman/Getty Images Sport/Getty Images, 21; Red Line Editorial, 22

Press Box Books, an imprint of Press Room Editions.

ISBN
978-1-63494-154-9 (library bound)
978-1-63494-167-9 (paperback)
978-1-63494-180-8 (epub)
978-1-63494-193-8 (hosted ebook)

Library of Congress Control Number: 2019951052

Distributed by North Star Editions, Inc.
2297 Waters Drive
Mendota Heights, MN 55120
www.northstareditions.com

Printed in the United States of America
012020

ABOUT THE AUTHOR

Brendan Flynn is a San Francisco resident and an author of numerous children's books. In addition to writing about sports, Flynn also enjoys competing in triathlons, Scrabble tournaments, and chili cook-offs.

TABLE OF CONTENTS

HAYES
11

CHAPTER 1

IN THE POST

The Houston Rockets began play in 1967 as the San Diego Rockets. They made the playoffs once in four seasons in San Diego. In 1971 they left California for Texas. It took more than two decades, but the Rockets broke through for their first NBA title in 1994.

They've had some incredible players along the way. Houston has long been known for excellent big men. The first of that group was **Elvin Hayes**. The "Big E" arrived in San Diego in the team's second year. He immediately made his mark, winning the NBA scoring title as a rookie.

In four seasons with the Rockets, Hayes averaged 27.4 points and 16.3 rebounds per game. His trademark move was a turnaround jumper. He also excelled on defense. The Rockets traded Hayes to Baltimore in 1972. The 12-time All-Star returned in 1981 to play three more seasons in Houston.

Rudy Tomjanovich spent all 11 years of his NBA career with the Rockets. He averaged a career-high 24.5 points per game in 1973–74. That was the first of five All-Star seasons for Tomjanovich.

COACH RUDY

Tomjanovich also spent eight and a half seasons as an assistant coach in Houston. Then he took over as head coach midway through the 1991–92 season. He stayed on through the 2002–03 season and led the Rockets to back-to-back NBA titles.

TOMJANOVICH
45
HOUSTON
45

Moses Malone was just 21 years old when he joined the Rockets in 1976. His Hall of Fame career took off in Houston. In six seasons there he averaged 24.0 points and 15.0 rebounds per game. He also won the first three of his six NBA rebounding titles with the Rockets.

Malone was strong. He was quick. And he had a nose for the ball like few others. He set an NBA single-game record with 21 offensive rebounds against Seattle in February 1982. He won the NBA Most Valuable Player (MVP) Award twice in Houston. And he powered the Rockets to their first NBA Finals in 1981.

MALONE
24

OLAJUWON
34
ROCKETS
34
EWING
33

Malone left Houston after winning the league MVP award in 1982. But he was soon replaced in the middle by another future Hall of Famer. Like Hayes, **Hakeem Olajuwon** had played college ball at the University of Houston. He became an instant fan favorite when the Rockets selected him first overall in the 1984 NBA Draft.

Already an elite athlete, Olajuwon worked to develop a dizzying array of low-post moves. He was a tenacious defender and a prolific scorer. He averaged more than 20 points per game in each of his first 13 NBA seasons.

STAT SPOTLIGHT

MOST CAREER REBOUNDS

ROCKETS TEAM RECORD

Hakeem Olajuwon: 13,382

In 1994 Olajuwon led the Rockets to their first NBA title. They won it again the next year too. He was named the Finals MVP both years.

Yao Ming's NBA career was the only thing about him that was relatively short. The 7'6" Yao joined the Rockets as the first overall pick of the 2002 draft. His transition from China to the United States was smooth. He quickly became an excellent shot blocker. He eventually developed a strong offensive game too. He scored a career-high 25.0 points per game in his fifth NBA season. Sadly, Yao was hampered by foot injuries that forced his early retirement at age 30.

YAO
11
ROCKETS
ROBINSON
50

MURPHY

23

STAT SPOTLIGHT

SINGLE-SEASON FREE-THROW PERCENTAGE

ROCKETS TEAM RECORD

Calvin Murphy: .958 (1980–81)

CHAPTER 2
BACKCOURT

The Rockets franchise has had a number of standout point guards who could also score. The first was **Calvin Murphy**. He spent all 13 years of his NBA career with the Rockets. Standing just 5'9", Murphy had an accurate jump shot and a willingness to drive to the hoop. He averaged at least 20 points per game in five seasons.

Murphy was perhaps best known for his success at the free-throw line. He once made 78 consecutive free throws. That stood as the NBA record for more than a decade.

Steve Francis was one of the flashier players in the NBA during his nine-year career. The Grizzlies drafted Francis second overall in 1999, but he forced a trade to Houston. He soon became known for his deadly

KENNY THE JET

Kenny Smith was the point guard on the Rockets' championship teams of the mid-90s. "The Jet" got his team off to a rousing start as they chased their second title. In Game 1 of the 1995 NBA Finals at Orlando, Smith made 7 of 11 three-pointers. The Rockets won in overtime and went on to sweep the Magic.

crossover dribble. It helped him get to the hoop and rack up free-throw attempts. Francis was a three-time All-Star with the Rockets before he was traded to Orlando in 2004.

HARDEN
13
ROKiT
HOUSTON
13
SPALDING

CHAPTER 3

MODERN STARS

The Rockets began to make deep runs in the Western Conference playoffs when **James Harden** arrived in 2012. The man known for his thick beard immediately took on the role of leading scorer for Houston. In 2018–19 he led the NBA in scoring for the second straight year, averaging 36.1 points per game.

An expert three-point shooter, Harden also gets to the free-throw line more than 10 times per game. And he does a lot of damage there too. He shot .861 from the line in his first seven seasons with the Rockets.

STAT SPOTLIGHT

SINGLE-SEASON THREE-POINTERS

ROCKETS TEAM RECORD

James Harden: 378 (2018–19)

Harden won the NBA MVP Award in 2017–18. The next year he was named to the All-NBA first team for the fifth time in his career.

Meanwhile, the Rockets made a bold move in July 2019. The team traded for point guard **Russell Westbrook**, one of the NBA's top players. Westbrook won

the 2016–17 NBA MVP Award for Oklahoma City when he led the league in scoring. He averaged a triple-double for the entire season. He again averaged a triple-double and led the NBA in assists the next two seasons. Along with young center **Clint Capela**, the Rockets have a trio of the game's most exciting players.

TIMELINE

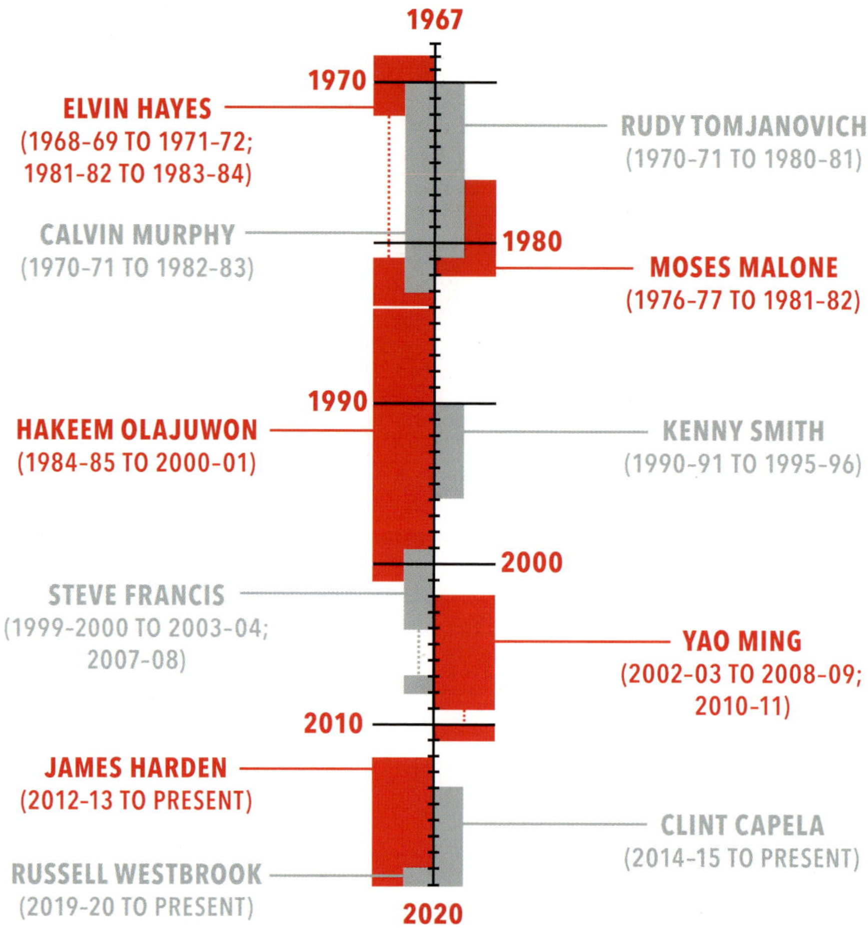
1967
1970
ELVIN HAYES
(1968-69 TO 1971-72;
1981-82 TO 1983-84)
RUDY TOMJANOVICH
(1970-71 TO 1980-81)
CALVIN MURPHY
(1970-71 TO 1982-83)
1980
MOSES MALONE
(1976-77 TO 1981-82)
1990
HAKEEM OLAJUWON
(1984-85 TO 2000-01)
KENNY SMITH
(1990-91 TO 1995-96)
2000
STEVE FRANCIS
(1999-2000 TO 2003-04;
2007-08)
YAO MING
(2002-03 TO 2008-09;
2010-11)
2010
JAMES HARDEN
(2012-13 TO PRESENT)
CLINT CAPELA
(2014-15 TO PRESENT)
RUSSELL WESTBROOK
(2019-20 TO PRESENT)
2020

TEAM FACTS

HOUSTON ROCKETS

Formerly: San Diego Rockets (1967–68 to 1970–71)

First season: 1967–68

NBA championships: 2*

Key coaches:

Mike D'Antoni (2016–17 to present)
173–73, 23–16 playoffs

Bill Fitch (1983–84 to 1987–88)
216–194, 21–18 playoffs

Rudy Tomjanovich (1991–92 to 2002–03)
503–397, 51–39 playoffs, 2 NBA titles

MORE INFORMATION

To learn more about the Houston Rockets, go to **pressboxbooks.com/AllAccess**.

These links are routinely monitored and updated to provide the most current information available.

**Through 2018–19 season*

GLOSSARY

crossover
A dribble that moves quickly from one hand to the other, allowing the ball handler space to drive to the hoop.

dizzying
Confusing, hard to track.

draft
A system that allows teams to acquire new players coming into a league.

offensive rebound
A rebound of a teammate's or one's own missed shot.

post
The area around the basket where power forwards and centers usually play.

prolific
Productive or plentiful.

rookie
A first-year player.

tenacious
Hard working, difficult to shake off.

triple-double
Accumulating 10 or more of three certain statistics in a game—usually points, rebounds, and assists.

turnaround
A shot that begins with the shooter's back to the basket.

INDEX